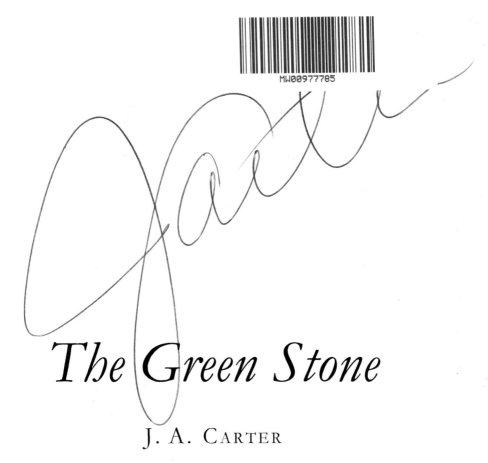

# The Green Stone

## J. A. CARTER

PublishAmerica
Baltimore

ISBN: 978-1-4489-2624-4 (softcover)
ISBN: 978-1-4489-9283-6 (hardcover)
PUBLISHED BY PUBLISHAMERICA, LLLP
www.publishamerica.com
Baltimore

Printed in the United States of America

*I would like to dedicate my first book to my sweet, precious grandmother, Alice Phillips, who influenced me to write. My adventures as a writer began when she held me in her arms and told me the most amazing stories that actually seem to come alive.*
*I miss and love you more than words can ever say!*

*I would like to thank my family for being supportive and at least "acting" like you loved my poems. Most of all, I would like to thank my dear husband for convincing me to finish my book and submit it for publishing. Without you I never would have had the confidence to fulfill this lifelong dream.*

J eronimo!" Sam yelled as he jumped from the dock. We were finally old enough to go down to the water with Sam's older brother, Billy. The water was still a little cool, but we were just excited to be away from school and summer chores. It was my turn to jump and I was a little nervous. I walked to the end of the dock and peeked over the edge. The water was clear and beautiful. I could see the bottom which was glittering white sand. Every now and then sand dollars, shells, and other small sea creatures floated by. In the middle of my peaceful daydream, I heard Billy's feet galloping behind me and suddenly my instincts told me to hold my breath. I hit the water on my side with Billy taking me in with him. "You snake! I am going to kick your tail." I was a pretty good swimmer and the water was so clear, I was able to catch him and dunk him twice before he reached up and pulled himself on the dock. This whole time Sam was busy catching crabs with his net. Most of the crabs were small and sort of cute, and they seemed to enjoy pinching us with their tiny pinchers. We spent the day splashing, swimming, exploring and watching Sam in his own little world, which was typical. He didn't have to talk a lot he was a thinker and you could tell his mind was always busy. It was almost time for us to get going when Sam called over for us to look at the huge crab he had caught. "You will never believe this! The crab has something caught in his claw." Billy and I ran over to see what he had found. "Hey Charli, is that a stone?" Billy asked me. "Yeah, I think it looks like part of the cliff that has broken off and is covered in seaweed." I replied. Yes, my name is Charli, spelled with an I and my two best friends are boys. "Sam, try to pry it out of his pinchers." Billy told him. He carefully pried the pinchers apart and took the rock. We stared as Sam cautiously wiped the seaweed from the stone. With the weeds wiped away, we were in awe from the beauty of the stone. It drew us in like some mysterious crystal ball only it was about the size of a gum ball. Could it be a real jewel or gem? We wondered. Were there more? At that very moment we swore on our friendships that it would be our secret and we would spend each day that summer hunting crabs and the treasures they may bring us. "Come on, guys. It's getting dark; we have to head back to the village." I said. The village, that's where we called home. We lived in a small town on a peninsula that was covered with lots of lush greenery. Our favorite part was the beach where we spent most of our time since we were born. At the beach was a large cliff that rose like a giant out into the beautiful green sea. We had grown up in the village and had never had a need to leave. Being one of the few girls, I had automatically been attached to Sam and Billy. I didn't care too much for being too "girly" right now, and they didn't seem to care either.

I didn't think I would ever sleep at all that night thinking about that mesmerizing green stone. Maybe we should research information on the village. Maybe there was a hidden treasure out in that lush green or maybe there was a report of some sunken ship that was carrying royal jewels. Sleep, it finally came at about three in the morning then abruptly ended when I awakened bright and early eager to run down the path to Sam's house. We just lived through the brush from each other, which was made up of huge exotic plants. I knocked on their back door and bit on a rolled up pancake, because my mom insisted that I eat something as I was trying to sneak away. Sam and Billy were both darting out the door just in time for Billy to snatch the last bite from my mouth. We walked through the village toward the cliff. After winding through the jungle's arms, we sat quietly in the soft white sand and watched the tide ease up to our toes. We sat silently for a while and I am sure thinking about the green stone. We put on our flippers, masks, grabbed our nets and eased in the water. We carefully netted half a dozen crabs and checked them for more treasure. We continued our search for the next few days with no luck. We gathered our stuff and walked back through the village. I eased away from the guys and slipped in one of my favorite shops, "The Candle Shop." I loved the aroma from the mixtures of burning candles. The shop was always dim; the only light came from the candles. The owner always gave me the creeps because she had shaggy grey hair, a couple of bad teeth, and wore a patch over one eye. She hardly ever spoke to customers and sometimes she didn't come out from behind the black curtain that divided the shop from whatever was behind it. I was also intrigued by the odd do-dads on display. She had odd looking little carvings on the shelves along with potions. Well, I don't know if they were potions but they looked like potions. They had strange names like, "Root Healer" and "Calming Potion." Sam and Billy yelled at me through the door, "Come on, weirdo!"

"Hey, I am coming." I replied. "Why do you like that place?" Sam asked me as I stepped out of the store. "I'm not sure, but I just feel drawn to it. Plus it smells good." I answered as we walked. "But, doesn't Madame Scary wig you out?" He continued. "Yeah, I guess sometimes but she hardly ever comes out and she acts like she doesn't even notice me." I answered. Billy jumped in and said, "The whole time she's probably planning on how she is going to boil your gizzard!" I giggled and added, "Shush!!! You're going to give Sam bad dreams." Sam reached over and frogged me on the arm and we ran the rest of the way home departing where the path split to each of our homes.

The funny thing was I couldn't think of anything else that night. I tossed and turned and eventually walked over to my bedroom window. The wind was blowing and things looked different, a little eerie. I stood there watching the trees thrash their spidery arms when "SMASH" a blackbird crashed into my window exactly where my face was. I tried to scream, but my throat was closing off and I just stood there frozen and waiting on something or someone to rescue me from my sudden state of shock. My lungs burned from the rush of air that finally was allowed to make its way down my throat. I sat down on the bed and tried to get my thoughts together. What just happened? Was it some kind of message? What made that crazy bird kill itself against my window? Maybe the wind was so strong that it caught the bird and blew it to its death. Needless to say, I did not sleep at all and thought morning would never come. I lay there as the sun peeked through the clouds and my heart pounded from the thoughts of the night before. Should I check on the remains of the bird? I decided that I would so I crept across my room and noticed the blood spatter on window. It took everything in me to keep walking to the window. I looked down and noticed the bird was gone. Sam! I thought. Could he have found a dead bird and thrown it at my window to scare the living daylights out of me? I couldn't imagine that he would be out that late at night by himself but it was the only way that I could justify what I had seen. If so, I would beat the crap out of him in about fifteen minutes. I quickly threw on some clothes, brushed my teeth, and took off out the door grabbing an apple on my way. "Sam, Sam." I yelled through the screen door. "Where are you?" He jumped out from the bushes and looked at me like I was crazy. "What is wrong with you, Charli?" He asked. "Like you don't know." I narrowed my eyes at him. "I swear that I don't know what you're talking about." He insisted. For some reason, I felt the hair stand up on the back of my neck. If Sam didn't do it, who did? What did? We sat on his porch steps and I told him step by step every detail of what happened. "Maybe the bird was delirious and flew into your window." He offered a more reasonable explanation after he noticed how upset I really was. "Maybe," I guessed that could be possible. Sam didn't want to show too much concern, so we grabbed our crab hunting equipment and took off to the cliff. When Billy got back from the general store, he joined us on our hunt for more treasure. It was a beautiful day and I felt better about the bird. We caught many crabs, but no stones. We decided that we may need to go out a little farther. There had been marks made in the side of the cliff to show us how far we were allowed to go. Did we dare go pass the marks? Billy was at the last mark when I remembered that I had promised Mrs. Prints that I would watch her seven year old daughter for a few hours while she went to play bingo. "Billy, I have to go babysit tonight. I forgot until just now." I called out to them. "Come on, Charli. We're here and we finally have our nerve worked up to pass the marks." I knew he was ill with me, but I had to go. "Tomorrow, we always have tomorrow. I have to go now or my mom will be mad if I make Mrs. Prints late for the game." All my mom had to do to really punish me was not let me go to the beach with the boys. "See you in the morning." I grabbed my stuff and took off back to the village. Something caught my eye. Something from a distance, something black. I slowed my pace, but kept walking through the town. I got closer and closer to the black then my feet wouldn't move. AHHH! It couldn't be! The black crow was hanging by its feet outside the candle shop. I was still stopped in my tracks when I noticed Ms. Byrtle was staring out the window with her one eye glaring at me. What did this mean? I finally forced my feet to move and I walked as fast as I could until I reached a small blue house with white shutters. Mrs. Prints was almost ready when I got there and she took only a few extra minutes to give me instructions that she knew that I already knew since I had been babysitting for her for at least a year. I had kept Jenni many times and she was easy because she loved playing in the yard. As I tossed a ball with her, I couldn't get the image of the dead bird out of my head. Could it be a different bird? Who was I kidding? Like crazy black birds decided to crash into windows all the time. The darker it got outside I knew that I had to quit thinking about it because I had to walk home after dark. Jenni and I went in for a snack and watched a movie until her mother arrived. Mrs. Prints paid me and I stepped out into the dark and headed home. My heart was thundering in my chest so I quickened my pace to jog. The village had that same eerie look as the night when the crow crashed in to my window. I began to feel sick and vomit tried to creep up my throat. I broke in to a run and could barely breathe when I rounded the corner of my house. I had never felt so relieved as when I stepped inside the door. Safe! Safe from what I didn't know.

I wasn't sure if I wanted to tell Sam and Billy but I knew I should. Billy always found a reason to tease me and I knew this would add fuel to the fire. Nothing scared Billy and he would probably think I was being a sissy. I met up with them the next morning and we headed for the cliff. I decided to enjoy the day and tell them later about the crow hanging upside down at the candle shop. We gathered our nets, masks, snorkels and flippers and began to swim pass the marks on the cliff. "I bet we'll catch larger crabs if we go out deeper," Sam said. It made sense that bigger crabs meant bigger stones. "Yeah, maybe we'll find out where the stone came from," I added. Suddenly, Billy came up for air and was yelling at us in excitement. "Look over here, you will not believe this!" We swam over as fast as we could. "What is it?" I asked. Billy was so excited he could barely speak. "Talk to me! What is it?" I demanded. He finally caught his breath and spoke, "It's a cave! An underwater cave." We both replied, "No way."

"Rest for a minute then go down about twenty feet and you will see a cave about three to four feet in diameter," Billy told us. I wasn't sure if I believed him, but I was dying to know. I took a deep breath and dived down. The cliff wall veered in at about fifteen feet and I felt my hand loose hold of the wall. I couldn't believe my eyes, and I couldn't hold my breath any longer. I turned and shot up to the surface. By the look on Sam's face, I knew he could tell that I had also found the cave. I didn't know what to say or think. There were so many strange things happening lately. First, it was the green stone, then the crow and now a cave. What could all of this mean? Were all these things connected? We needed to figure out how to stay down there long enough to see how deep it was. We swam back to shore and lay on the hot sand resting and trying to come up with a plan. How could we get down there faster and still have time to see if the cave was really a deep cave or just a place where the water had worn a hole in the cliff. After what seemed like hours of sitting and just thinking, we came up with a plan that we thought might work. We had to make a longer snorkel. Billy decided to head back to home for a machete, while Sam and I hunted for bamboo. We searched carefully to find a bamboo that was really long but small enough to fit tightly around our snorkels. By the time we found a few stalks that we thought would work, Billy was back ready to cut one down. We had to cut a few before we found one that was tight enough not to allow water to seep in our mouths. Since Billy found the cave, he volunteered to go first. He took a deep breath and dove down pulling on the pole to add speed to his dive. We knew that he had reached the snorkel because water blew out the top of the bamboo. As we waited to see what Billy had found, Sam took out the green stone. We stared at it in awe. There seemed to be something magical about the stone something that drew us in and kept us captivated. Finally breaking our stare I asked, "Where is Billy? I don't hear him breathing through the bamboo."

"Oh gosh. Billy isn't breathing?" Sam looked at me. "Maybe he is looking around the cave and coming back and forth for air." I tried to comfort him, but I knew that I was getting worried too. "No, Charli he hasn't been back for air since I pulled out the stone. We have to check on him." He said. "Oh, alright. I will go check on Billy." I said as I took in as much air, adjusted my mask, and dove down as quickly as I could. When I reached the bottom of the bamboo I went straight to the snorkel and blew carefully before I took in new air. My heart was pounding as I searched around for Billy. I wanted to yell his name, but obviously I couldn't. I got enough air to leave the bamboo, and felt my way to the deep part of the cave. Suddenly I felt like I was being sucked through a tunnel. The water was passing so quickly that it stung my skin. I couldn't see or think, things were happening so rapidly and I realized that I couldn't breathe. I was drifting away becoming unconscious, at the same time I wanted to scream for help then someone grabbed by arm and pulled me to the surface. It all went black. I don't know how long I was out but I remember awakening with water and vomit coming up my throat. The next thing I remember was the smell. It was a smell of rot and death. My mind was trying to make my eyes open heard coughing and gagging beside me. I turned and peered through tiny slits of my eyes to see Billy and Sam coughing. I was alive! We were alive! Billy was looking at me with a strange look on his face. Was it fear? "What's wrong, Billy?" I asked. "I thought I was dead, and I thought you and Sam were dead too." He answered. "I know. We were so worried about you. What just happened?"

"I guess the suction pulled us through the tunnel and we ended up in this huge open cave." He told us. "What about the smell? Where is it coming from?" I continued to ask. "It's probably dead fish that get caught in here with the rising and falling of the tide." I was amazed at how grown up Billy sounded sometimes even though he was only one year older than me. At sixteen, he was very responsible and reasonable. Sam answered my question with a sudden gasp. He scrambled back on his hands and bottom like a crab. I couldn't see over the rock protruding out of the water because I was still sitting on a flat rock where I had come up from. Sam had eased his way around the rock and saw something that had obviously sent him to scrambling back to us. "What is it? What did you see?" He didn't answer. All he could do was point. Billy and I reluctantly eased our way toward Sam and immediately went running back across the rocks. I ended up in Billy's arms trembling from the sight of three human skeletons. There were three skulls that looked like they had surely died a dreadful death. Their mouths were open and distorted as if they were yelling and begging for their lives. I had a sick feeling that we were somewhere we shouldn't be. I couldn't stop trembling. We were all trembling, even Billy. There were so many questions and we didn't know where to begin and who would we ask. First, we decided that we needed rest. We would never make it back through the tunnel in our condition, much less state of mind. "Come on, let's climb up the rocks and get dry." Billy finally said. "What if the tide rises and we get trapped? We will drown." Sam asked. "Don't talk like that. We have to stay positive. Plus, look at the old water line on the cave wall. It only goes up a little higher. We have plenty of room up there on the ledge. Start climbing." He commanded. We both automatically looked to Billy as our leader. Without a word, we began climbing until we reached the ledge. We sat in a close huddle until we all drifted off to sleep. It came easily and I don't know how long we slept until a loud explosion jolted us to a stand. We naturally grabbed hold of each other. "What the heck was that?" Sam asked. Before either of us could answer him another explosion shook the inside of the cave. Instinct told us to run. We were not sure where to run, but we followed Billy into a larger tunnel. For some reason, I felt that we were running toward the explosion but we didn't have any idea where we were going. We were running so fast that we didn't even realize the tunnel had come to an end and we dropped so quickly that it took my stomach. We were clawing at water as we dropped and finally reached the surface of a body of water that stretched as far as the eyes could see. Another explosion sent rocks showering around us. We were in the middle of a bad dream. Worse, it was a nightmare. There were two ships shooting at each other. One of the ships looked old, but powerful and the other looked like one that may carry goods to and from other countries. There were men on the ships yelling orders and shooting at each other. We didn't have time to think, because we were being showered with huge rocks again. We had to find safety and find it now. At the same time, we swam the opposite way of the ships to what looked like an island. By the time we got to shore, I thought my chest would cave in. "My legs are cramping and my chest is burning." I cried. Billy and Sam each grabbed an arm and carried me to cover. I felt tears streaming down my face. I wasn't the crying kind of girl, but my body hurt and I was scared. The men on the ships had not noticed us because they were too busy fighting and shooting at each other. NO! We could not be in a pirate story. We didn't even know where we were. We didn't even know this existed on the other side of our cliff. I didn't understand what was happening or why. All I knew was that we had been sucked through the tunnel and swam to an island that we had never seen. We sat and watched the fighting for an hour until a strange sound caught our attention. Silence! The fighting stopped and the men on the older ship boarded the other one. There were a few men left on the ship with their hands high above their heads. We heard loud outrageous laughs coming from the men holding them hostage, and the next sounds were screams as swords pierced their sides. The ship was raided and the men went back to their ship with the goods. "Charli, we have to come up with a plan. What if they come to shore? We must start searching this island for some place to hide." Billy was holding it together for all of us. Sam was even more quiet than usual. "Let's go. We had to find a hiding place where we could still see the ship. We followed him deeper in to the jungle for thicker coverage, but where we could still keep an eye on the ship. Even though we weren't thinking about food, we noticed there was plenty of fruit available. We began gathering large plant leaves, bamboo, and limbs to build a crude shelter. The only problem would be water. We knew that we couldn't drink salt water and the only way would be to boil it, but that would mean a fire. A fire would lead to smoke and smoke would lead a trail to us. "The fruit will provide us with fluids. We can drink whatever juice we can get from the fruit." I offered. Billy didn't answer but smiled with approval. With that solved we concentrated on our shelter. The sun began to hide behind the trees which told us we had worked diligently not noticing that night was on its way. We all stopped and realized at the same time that we had to find some kind of food before dark. The boys went hunting while I stayed behind and made beds for us and kept watch over the ship. They returned just before it was completely dark and we sat and shared whatever food we had. As we sat huddled together in our small shelter, the noises of night began to come alive. Water swishing and creatures moving was enough to tighten our huddle and quicken our heart beats. We didn't know what was worse, the men on the ship or the creatures that were prowling around us. As night swelled around us, it seemed the voices got louder and the animals seemed to ease closer. "One of us must stay awake at all times. We will take turns keeping watch while the other two rest." Billy said. "I couldn't sleep if I wanted to, so I don't mind going first. As soon as I start getting too sleepy, I will awaken one of you." I offered. Sam and Billy laid down to rest and I watched quietly as the boat rocked back and forth like a giant baby in its gentle crib. I don't know how long I kept watch, but it must have been enough time for Billy to trade out with me. He crawled over and tapped me on the shoulder. "Hey, you go get some rest. I can watch for a while." He whispered. I didn't answer I just turned and took his spot on the little crude bed of plant leaves. I don't know when I actually fell asleep, but the next thing I knew the sun was piercing through the leaves and the morning critters were chatting back and forth. They were probably fussing about us interrupting their homes. I rolled over to notice Sam and Billy were both sleeping. I guess the night watch didn't last past me. "Hey guys, wake up." I nudged them. They both bolted straight up. "What? Huh? What is it?" They were still disoriented from being suddenly awakened. "Nothing, I just thought we should get up since the day has started without us." I said teasingly. They knew that I was right so they tried adjusting their eyes to the sun. "I am going to walk a little ways over here and if I am not back in three minutes come looking for me." I told them. They didn't ask any questions. I guess they knew that Mother Nature was calling. I took care of my business and gave them a chance to do the same. "Other than that kind of business, I think we should stay together at all times." Sam said. We agreed and eased our way through plants, flowers, trees, and vines until we reached an opening big enough to really see the men on the ship without them seeing us. The sight was breathtaking. It looked like a black shiny stone resting peacefully on the rolling green blanket of sea. We stood there not really knowing what to do. Are they still on the ship? Sam asked. "Yes, I'm sure they are still asleep. They were up all night singing, shooting and whatever." Billy confirmed. "Good, maybe this will give us some time to figure out a plan. Food was first on our list so we browsed around and found something to eat. Whether we liked it or not, we knew that we needed to keep our strength in case the ship moved closer to us. We stayed close to our shelter and gathered as much as we could carry. We spent most of the morning eating fruit and drinking the juice. "Should we swim back to the cave?" I asked during breakfast. "No way. The men will see us. The only reason they didn't see us before is because they were fighting. We will have to wait till they leave." Billy turned to us to say. "But what if they don't leave?" Sam asked. Once again we relied on Billy to be strong and get us through this. "They will have to eventually. Sailors sail! They will have to eat." He explained. We all stopped eating and looked up at each other. Oh no, that made us think that they may have to come to shore after all. Billy assured us that sailors lived by having the wind in their faces, fishing and they were probably stocked up with goods. We convinced ourselves to believe him for the time being, at least. To keep busy, we searched the island but didn't venture too far away from our shelter. The island looked the same all over and we didn't want to get lost. We inched our way through the brush to where it met sand. It was a great feeling when our feet hit the warm sun, but we refrained from getting too excited because we didn't want to draw attention to ourselves. "Come on, let's just walk around the edge of the beach and see how far it goes this way." Billy said as he pointed to his left. We walked for what seemed like ours when we were stopped dead in our tracks by voices. We immediately crouched in the brush and watched. We couldn't believe what we were witnessing. There were men, obviously from the ship, digging a hole. It was a hole big enough for a body. Whose body? We stayed as still as possible trying not to breathe. Billy motioned for us to lie down and crawl backwards which we immediately obeyed. Whatever was going on, we didn't want to know or see. When we felt we were far enough away we ran as fast as we could until we reached our shelter. We lay motionless forever it seemed. "Billy, they're on the island. They came to shore and we never knew it." I said with tears building in my eyes. "I know." He answered with what may have been tears in his own eyes. When we thought it couldn't get worse, it did. "Did you notice the odd way they spoke? What language was that?" I added more panic to the conversation. "Yeah, I noticed that and I don't have an answer for you. I do know that we have to find our way back to the cave and back home tonight." I glanced back at Sam and noticed the frantic look on his face. Sam stared blankly at the ground and looked lost. I looked at Billy and he too had noticed Sam's silence and fear. We put everything else aside and talked to Sam first. "Sam, are you ok?" He looked up at us and burst into tears. I reached out and grabbed him and hugged him until he calmed down. "Look, we are all scared, but we can't break down. We have to work together to get out of here." I tried to comfort him. He nodded in agreement and turned away from us. "We will keep watch and get out of here tonight." Billy added. Would night ever get here? The sun barely peeked over the horizon and we waited anxiously for the shadow of the night. "Come on, let's ease into the water and make our way back to the cave." Billy said once night arrived. "The ship has come alive so they must be back to their celebrations." We quietly followed him to the water and waded out until we were unable to touch the bottom. I noticed large ripples coming toward us. It wasn't a normal wave caused by the tilt of the moon, but something different. Billy and Sam had stopped swimming, too. "Did you guys see that?" I asked. Before they could answer another swirl came toward us. We joined together back to back. Something swirled around us then and Sam yelled. We turned to see him disappear under the water. Oh gosh, where did he go? My mind screamed. It was huge and it was all around us and worst of all, it had Sam. "Sam, Sam." We yelled as we searched the water. I was so tired and had to get back to shore. "We can't go on without him. We have to swim back to shore and keep yelling for him." Billy demanded with a mix of anger and fear in his voice. He was nowhere to be seen, he was gone. We saw more swirling in the water and Billy ran, jumped, swam toward it but was unable to see Sam. By this time, I was crying, really crying and I didn't care if Billy noticed. Actually, I think he was crying too. We stayed awake all night searching the waters for Sam, until the heat of the morning was waking and scorching everything it touched. My eyes were obviously swollen and I strained to see across the water. Suddenly, a glint of blue caught my eye. I grabbed Billy's arm. "Billy, look! What is that?" We both strained our eyes to see that Sam had washed ashore. We ran frantically around the bend in the cove toward the blue speck which turned into Sam's shirt. Blue and Red! Blue and Red! One leg was covered in blood. We fell at his side and began to check over him. Was he alive? Why was he bleeding? He was unconscious and didn't respond when we turned him on his side to try to clear the water from his throat. We knew what we must do, CPR. Our parents had made us attend first aid training for life guards last year, so we were familiar with some things that must be done immediately. Plus, we were all that he had. If we didn't try anything, he could die. Billy pressed on his chest as I counted, then I breathed into his mouth while Billy counted. We continued this over and over until finally Sam coughed and choked up black and green fluid. "We did it! He's going to be ok!" We hugged him so tightly that we were squeezing the air out of him. We pushed him back and just looked at him while he focused his eyes. He was still coughing up the gross yuck, then he looked at us and tried to give us a tiny grin. "Oh, thank God. You're bleeding a little, so we need to check that before we get too far from the water. Are you feeling well enough for us to wash it off?" He nodded his head so we cupped water in our hands and washed most of the blood off of his leg. Once it was clean, I grabbed his legs and Billy lifted his upper body and we carried him back to our little shelter. It took us a while because we had to take a few steps at a time then rest. We finally got him back and laid him down on the bed of leaves. I began cleaning his leg again while Billy got him to drink some juice from a fresh fruit. When Sam laid back and closed his eyes, I motioned for Billy to look at his leg. He had major gashes and a few chunks of meat missing from his calf. We started cleaning and tore pieces of Billy's shirt and tied it around the worst wounds. We didn't want to tie it too tight because we didn't want to completely stop circulation to the rest of his leg, but we had to keep it clean and covered. He slept while we wrapped giant plant leaves around his leg hoping this would at least keep him from losing too much blood. After about an hour, we lay down next to him and couldn't stop the sleep from taking over. We had been awake for about two days and our bodies had given in. We slept.

The next day, I awakened feeling unusually warm. The extra warmth didn't come from the sun, but from Sam's body. He was between us and obviously had a fever. I noticed that Billy was gone. I stood, stretched and tried to recall what my mom had done when I had a fever. Fluids, he had to have fluids. Billy returned with an armful of fruit and a really worried look on his face. "He's sick, Charli. He has developed a fever, probably from an infection in his leg." His voice dragged as he spoke like he didn't know if he could take much more, but he did. He was being so strong and taking care of all of us. "I know. I will try to get him to drink if you want to change his leg wrap." He nodded and headed to the water with a giant leaf. I lifted his upper body and leaned him against me as I squeezed some of the juice into his mouth. He sort of choked at first then accepted the juice like a starving animal. He was so weak, but tried hard to do what we asked of him. Billy was back and washing his leg and he moaned in pain. His wound was really gross and I gagged a few times when the wrenching smell of blood and pus reached my nostrils. When we finished cleaning him we decided to let it get some fresh air for a little while before we bandaged it back. Billy spent the afternoon pacing the beach. I knew he was worried and thinking of a way to get home. He came back to the shelter right before the sun dipped below the horizon. "One of us must go back and get help. I want to but I am scared to leave you here alone with him. There's more danger here than back home." He suggested. "You know that I can. I just need to take a few minutes to back track and remember how we came." I said with confidence yet I really wasn't sure I could get back. We sat on the beach and traced a map in the sand. I knew I had to swim back to the cliff, but when we ran through the tunnel, we dropped God knows how far before we hit water. That meant that I had to find another way home. Right before dark, I kissed Sam on the forehead and turned to Billy. Before I knew it, he had me wrapped in his arms. "You can do this, Charli. You are the toughest girl that I know and I have faith that you will make it home for help." To make light of the situation, I said, "I am one of the only girls that you know." I turned and eased out into the water. I took my time because I knew I had a long ways to swim and I had no idea what I would do when I got to the cliff. I took soft strokes and concentrated on how I would get in because I didn't want to think about the men on the ship or the monster below me that swirled the water right here a few nights before. My eyes were constantly casing the cliff for an opening. It felt like I would never reach it, then finally I found a rock to hang on to. My arms and legs were suffering with sharp pains. I rested for a few minutes before I decided to start looking for an opening. I turned and glanced back at the island and noticed Billy was still watching me. I gave him a quick wave to let him know that I was fine and he seemed to give me a shy wave back. I took a few deep breaths and hoped that I would find an underwater cave just like the one we came through. I searched for a long while taking breaks on the rock that I found when I finally found an opening. This was my chance, so I said a quick prayer and entered the dark cave. That rushing feeling came again as I was being sucked in through the tunnel. I didn't panic because I knew, at least I hoped that I knew, that some magical force would suck me through and I would come up feeling horrible but I would be alive. My eyes and throat were taking in water. I was pulling and kicking trying to get to the surface because I knew Billy would not be on the other side to pull me out like before. My fingers clawed the rocky dirt and my lungs felt like they were on fire. I didn't think that I had the strength to pull myself up but I made it half way out of the water and just stayed there for awhile. Slimy water made its way up my throat until I threw it all up. When I had enough energy, I pulled myself completely out of the water. I made it! I had actually made it to the cave. I climbed to a higher point in case the water rose again. I slept and dreamed. Flashes of the black crow, blood splattered on my window, and the old woman. The old woman was pointing at me and she was mouthing something through those bad teeth. What was she trying to tell me or what was she yelling at me? My mind was trying to wake me up while I begged for more sleep. I wanted to finish my dream, but my brain pulled my eyes open and I slowly gained consciousness. I sat up and my whole body ached. I rolled my head around to loosen my muscles and looked around the cave trying to decide how to get out. I still had a journey ahead and didn't have time to waste. I didn't see a long tunnel to run through like we did before. Oh, I had to find a way. I knew Sam needed me to get help quickly. The cave was huge and I wasn't sure where to begin, but I got up and started looking for any tunnel that I thought might lead me back home. So I picked a small entrance that looked like the one the old woman was pointing at in my dream. I pushed that from my mind and started running. "Oh gosh, I am trapped!" I said aloud. Suddenly, I dropped and my stomach caught in my throat and a flowing current pushed me out into familiar territory. "I made it!" I yelled aloud and my voice was one of the best sounds that I had heard in a long time. I swam to that wonderful shore that Sam and Billy had played on since we were born. I wanted to roll around in the warm sand, but I knew that I didn't have time so I crept through the path to the village. I didn't even have time to let our parents know what was going on, so I decided that I would have to sneak through the village to my house. My first thought was 'dry clothes' so I ran straight to my room and changed clothes. After changing, I grabbed a snack and was back out the door in just a few minutes. I went the back way to town to try to get some medicine for Sam. As I wearily passed The Candle Shop, I stopped because Ms. Byrtle was pointing at me and saying something that I couldn't understand. I found that I couldn't stop myself from walking straight to her like I was in a trance. She was still pointing at me when I got to the front door of the shop. I stepped inside and her voice actually began to form these words, "Don't go back to the cave. Danger awaits there." Her voice made me think that she was concerned. Before I could answer, she disappeared to the back of the store. "Wait!" I yelled. "Please, I need help. My friend is sick. I have to go back to the cave. Please! We can't tell anyone because they may not let me go back and he could die if I don't get medicine." I kept pleading for help as I walked to the back of the store and through the black curtain. The smell went from a mixture of candles to musty dirt. I could barely see anything and I tried to give my eyes time to focus. There were tiny bottles on the shelves filled with colored liquids. There were other bottles filled with what looked like creatures or parts of creatures. I noticed a small table in the corner with a bottle and a note. The note was scribbled, "Go in haste, you are in great danger!" I stuffed the bottle in my pocket and took off before someone else came in the store. I shot out the door and turned to go off the porch when I ran straight into the crow. I made a yelping noise and stumbled backwards. I got myself together and stared at the crow as it was spinning on a string. I still didn't understand what was going on, but I did know that I had to get back to Sam. My feet hit the water and I swam out past the marker, took a deep breath, and dove as deep as I could. With all the adrenaline that was built up inside of me, I didn't have any problem diving deep enough to find the cave. I followed my hand to the cave and before I could express any dread about what was fixing to happen, it happened. I was drawn in to the tunnel. The suction and pull took my breath each time where I didn't feel like I could ever get use to it. I lay on the rocks, gulping up water and trying to find the strength to get back to the boys. I checked my pockets for the bag of medicine and felt that it was safe. I lay there staring at the walls of the cave and slowly drifted to sleep. I felt my body trying to wake up, but I was so stiff from lying on the rock. I leaned down and rubbed my legs to get the blood circulating. I stood and began walking toward the tunnel. I decided to jog because I thought it would make the fall a little easier. Once again, I couldn't ever get use to the ground suddenly disappearing out from under me. My stomach jumped again and I hit the water. I came up and waded a few minutes before I made the long swim to shore. I took my time swimming, but tried to stay aware of everything around me. Reaching the shore was one of the greatest feelings of my life, especially when Billy ran out to meet me. "Charli, you made it back. Are you ok? I know it was hard, but you did it, girl. Did you get medicine?"

"I did and you don't even want to know who helped me. How is he?" I asked as we walked back to the crude little shelter where Sam laid waiting. "He's not so well and he is still burning hot. He has been vomiting since you left. His leg is still pouring pus, so I have been trying to keep it as clean as possible. Even though I have been forcing him to drink, he doesn't seem to be getting better." I noticed that tears were forming in his eyes, so I decided to change the subject. I began by telling him how I got the medicine from Madam Scary, as he calls her. "I can't explain her actions but she gave me this bottle of liquid and then gave me this horrible warning of how dangerous this place is. Like we don't know the danger we are in. How did she even know we are here or anything about this place? I wanted to ask her, but she disappeared and I left immediately. I took the bottle because I knew that I didn't want anyone else to see me and I didn't have any other choice. We just have to trust her." Billy agreed and added, "I can't believe she helped you. Why?"

"I don't know but she told me not to come back and I explained that Sam was very sick. She went away and left a note with the medicine so here I am." I finished most of the story by the time we reached Sam and he was babbling in his sleep. Tears welled up in my eyes when I saw him because it was obvious that he had worsened. I dropped to my knees and felt of his head. It burned to the touch and I took the medicine out of my pocket. "Billy, hold his head up while I pour some into his mouth." Before I finished he already had Sam in his arms and was opening his mouth. I poured two capfuls into his mouth and we tilted his head back to make sure all the medicine made it all the way down. He continued to babble, so we just laid him back down and began to work on his leg. It was still oozing pus which was probably the source of his fever. When I pulled the final leaf I felt it hold on to some meat which meant part of his wound may be scabbing over, healing. I didn't realize how exhausted I was until I lay on the bed of leaves beside Sam. I felt my body fall quickly in to a deep sleep. Days passed and Billy and I nursed Sam the best we knew how. The fourth day, he wanted to get up and help us around our shelter, but we reminded him of the pus draining from his leg and the pain in the butt he had been. He sat in the sand and pouted while we tried to catch some small sea creatures. We had been eating fruit for over a week now and we needed something more. "I don't really think we should wade out too far. There is something in that water and until we have to, I say we stay close to shore." I suggested. "I agree. I found plenty of crabs and mussels being pushed in by the waves. We can have a small feast on these if we get to fishing." He told me. We scooped up as many of the small creatures that we could and headed back to the shelter. Billy grabbed my arm and said, "Look, the ship is gone!" We automatically looked around us as far as we could see and the ship was nowhere to be found. "Where do you think it could be?" I turned toward him for his answer. "I'm not sure, but I am sure that it will be back. Let's take advantage of it being gone and build a fire to cook our supper." That sounded great because we had not had anything cooked in so long, well at least a week but it felt like forever. We broke off some dry limbs and carried them back to get a fire started.

We carefully made a pile and crumbled some dry leaves to get it started. He took his watch face off and let the sun reflect through the glass. We had gotten in trouble for this many times at home, so we were pretty experienced at being pyromaniacs. After a while, the dried leaves began to smoke and started igniting. We carried the small ball of flames to the shelter where we had a pile ready. After we had a decent fire going, he threw the shells in and let them cook until they popped open. We don't know if it was because we were starving or what, but it tasted awesome. We used the fruit as drinks and enjoyed our fireside supper like we were at some fancy restaurant. After feasting on our seafood, we tried to come up with another plan to escape the island. Sam brought the green stone out of his pocket and it seemed like every time we saw it was the first time. We sat and stared at it for a while until Billy said, "You know, that green stone was the beginning of our trouble."

"Yeah, I know but for some reason I don't think we should get rid of it." They both nodded. We sat there quietly and watched the fire burn down slowly. We weren't sure if the ship would come back, but Billy felt that it had some important reason for being near this island. "So, what's the plan?" I asked as I watched him sit in deep thought. "Since Sam is feeling a little better, we must find a way to get away before the ship returns." Before I could answer Sam jumped in, "I am not going anywhere near that water. Whatever cut my leg open is big and dangerous. I am too scared to go back in there."

"I understand how you feel, and I had time to think about it while you were sick. We can either build a raft or steal a small boat from the ship if it comes back." Billy suggested. "Oh, I think I would rather work on building a raft." I said. "Tomorrow we will begin gathering bamboo and any dry sticks that we can find. We need to get some rest and pray the ship doesn't come back for a couple of days." With that said we all laid down and tried to rest. I didn't go to sleep from thinking about Ms. Byrtle. Whatever she gave me helped Sam. He may have died without it with such a horrible infection and high fever. Even though, he was still weak and had to be careful we knew he was on the road to recovery. I couldn't help but wonder how we would ever get his body back home if he didn't make it. Stop! I couldn't think negative thoughts. I had to think positively.

I finally slept and dreamed of Ms. Byrtle. She was pointing at me and saying something that I desperately wanted to hear, but my dream state wouldn't let me. Her hand seemed to stretch out to me and grab my shoulder. She started shaking me and I slowly began to wake up with Sam being the one that was actually shaking me awake. "Come on, Charli. Wake up! What are you dreaming, because you are moaning something crazy?" I wasn't ready to tell them about my dreams so I just told him that I didn't know. I stretched and stood up ready to get started on our raft. We gathered some sturdy bamboo and tore some vines to hold the raft together. It took most of the day since we had to go deeper into the island to find better wood. Sam waited at the edge of the jungle each time so that we wouldn't get lost. With enough wood, we went back to the beach near the shelter and dropped the last of our supplies. We ate, rested and made plans to leave out on the raft early in the morning. I decided to start a small fire before we settled in for the night. I collected small pieces of wood and twigs and within a few minutes I got it to ignite. I added a few pieces at a time being careful not to smother the flames. Just watching the dancing flames put me in a sleepy trance. I fought sleep from fear of bad dreams, but was eventually overcome with fatigue. The smell was like that of dead rotting flesh. It was dark, pitch black and the smell got stronger. Obviously we had all slept so soundly that we had let the fire go out sometime during the night. There was a movement, a presence close by. I laid still. I was completely frozen by fear. I couldn't tell if Billy and Sam were awake but I knew they weren't moving either. I lay there as the smell filled my nostrils, and I felt vomit rise up my throat. I knew that I couldn't throw up so I tried to swallow it and held my breath. Softly, I felt Sam grab my hand and I knew he also sensed something was there. Suddenly, Billy jumped up and started yelling and running. Two dark figures started running after him. We knew that Billy was trying to divert the intruders away from us, but we couldn't let them hurt him either. We were in this together no matter what. "Come on, Sam. We have to help." I whispered. We eased our way toward the sound of Billy yelling when we were grabbed. My heart almost leapt out of my chest. We were caught by what or whom we didn't know, but it was the source of that horrible smell that had awakened me. I kicked, screamed, and bit the stinking beast until a sharp pain shot through the back of my head. I was a little dazed and confused with my head still stinging, but I could tell that I was being dragged across wet sand. Since the source of the stinging was coming from being dragged by my hair, I didn't fight anymore. I eventually lost consciousness for an unknown length of time until I was slowly awakened by strange voices. They were standing around us talking and laughing. The giant blue sea swirled around me spinning and spinning. My head ached and acid burned my throat until I couldn't hold it any longer. My stomach contracted and pushed until it finally tore out my mouth. Since I was on my back some of the chunks tried to go back down and I began choking on my own puke. My mind was telling me to wake up as I was trying to regain complete consciousness, because I managed to roll over on my side. I finished being sick, but still had a massive headache. The voices were distant, but I could feel them watching me. Where were Sam and Billy? I had not heard or seen them since I was wacked in the head. I am not sure how long I fought sleep, because I was scared that I would fall unconscious once again. I couldn't stop it. I was out, sound asleep. Pain, pain screamed throughout my body and that was how I woke up much later to the sun setting across the sea. Across the sea? Was I rocking back and forth? No, I couldn't be aboard their ship. My breathing suddenly became rapid and my chest heaved. "Sam, Billy are you here?" My voice was raspy from the sun baking the back of my throat. Even a whisper was hard to hear and I had to spit to make it better. I heard a quiet moan coming from not too far away. I realized it was Billy. He slowly turned his head toward me and I knew he was hurting as bad as I was. "Where is Sam?" He barely got out. "I don't know I just woke up myself. This doesn't look good. We are in a lot of trouble..." Before I could finish what I was saying I was lifted up from behind. I was face down with my arms around my back and it felt like they were being pulled out of their sockets. We were set on our feet and pushed to one side of the ship to face our adversaries. Many nasty men stared at us. Some of them with smirks and some had no expressions at all. Still, we didn't see any sign of Sam. "Where is our friend?" I yelled. "Shut up! You only speak when spoken to." One of them stepped toward me showing his authority. "Where is he?" I demanded. I tensed waiting for the big man in charge to slap me or something then I felt Billy step toward us. Two of the other men grabbed him and slung him across the deck. "You need to learn to keep your mouth shut, girlie, or I will have to shut it for you." I was too scared to even scream but I had learned a lesson at that moment. If not for own safety, I had to keep my mouth shut for Billy. He would get hurt defending me and I wouldn't be able to live with myself if I caused him any harm. I looked over at him to let him know that I was sorry and I could see the anger shooting out of his eyes like arrows from a bow. I stared at him until he made eye contact with me and we both knew without any words that we had to plan smarter if we were going to survive this. Being in the middle of the ocean would prove to be a harder task than we could ever imagine but we weren't about to give up now. With no land in sight, it would be next to possible to make it to land without lots of patience. "Girlie, what are you doing out here all alone? Are you looking for something special?" I immediately looked at Billy and knew he didn't want me to say anything about the stone, much less that it was in Sam's pocket. Sam, oh gosh, where was he? Please be ok, Sam. We knew that he was still weak from the creature and that the infection would get worse if it wasn't kept clean. I didn't answer the man and he seemed to accept that for now. There was nowhere to go and nothing to do but watch them bustle about the ship so Billy and I used this time to actually communicate for the first time. "What do you think is so important that they were asking me about?" I whispered. "I don't know, but we have to find out what it is. That could be our ticket out of here." He whispered back. "Yeah, whatever it is, it means kidnapping and killing is worth it to them." I added as we watched the sun set and the ship rocked us both to sleep. Morning came with my lips cracked and swollen from the sun and wind. The men were scurrying around the ship when one of them spoke to us with that strange accent. He obviously said something about food because he tossed us each a strip of meat, sort of like jerky. I looked at Billy for approval and he was already chewing on the offering of protein. It wasn't the greatest taste, but it was food. There was something different this morning and I stopped chewing as he jumped up and looked over the railing. "Land, we are anchored. They are lowering a couple of boats to take to shore. We have to play this smart. Land may be our first step to freedom." We ate the slop they served us and watched the men steadily work. They piled into boats and rowed to shore. The land they were heading toward looked like any other island, a lush green monster. It was huge and its beauty could take your breath away. It was also full of danger. "We will have to be patient before we decide to get to the island because we may never get home." I knew he was right, but it was so hard to wait when we were so desperate to go home. We heard shuffling behind us and turned to see a few of the men climbing over the side of the ship. They were walking towards us and mumbling words that I couldn't understand, but it was obviously about us. "Get up!" The big man who seemed to take charge again ordered us. He didn't look like he was the highest person on this vessel, but he was definitely in charge of us. We stood up out of fear and to make sure we didn't make him mad. "We're going to shore." He ordered. "What about our friend? Where is he? He is very sick and needs attention." I said. "We know that he is sick, and we are keeping him down below. We have someone checking on him and cleaning his wound." He answered as if I had insulted them. I had to change tactics. I couldn't be bossy. I had to seem humble and weak. "Please, may we see him? Please, they are brothers and we haven't seen him in two days." I could tell that he was thinking about what I said then replied, "No one is allowed down below without permission or by themselves." Before he could say no I broke in, "You can take us and stay with us just let us see him."

"Well, I don't know." One of the other men leaned in to the big man and said, "Go on, Mullet. What's it going to hurt? Just get it over with then we don't have to listen to their whining for the rest of the day." Mullet turned and motioned for us to follow. He led us below deck, down a narrow stairway and through a hall that held rooms on each side. Finally, Mullet stopped in front of one of the doors and looked back at us. I guess he was making sure we knew he was still in charge of the situation. What he didn't know is that we were taking in every inch of our surroundings and burning it into our memories. We looked back at him innocently as he nodded and opened the door. We entered the third room on the left and saw Sam. The sight of him caused a small lump to rise in my throat and I knew Billy was feeling the same kind of lump. Sam was lying in a small bed very limp, but he was alive. We walked over to him as Mullet stood at the door watching our every move. As we turned back to Sam, he slowly opened his eyes. I reached for his hand and he smiled at me weakly "Hey guys! Where you two been?" He struggled to say. He tried to add a laugh, but winced in pain. "Water, thirsty." He said through that familiar scratchy voice that I experienced when I had first awakened. We turned to Mullet expecting him to get some water. "I'm going to lock you in here so don't try anything funny." He said as he left to fetch some water. The room was bare except for Sam and the bed. Surprisingly, it was very clean. We had no idea how we could possibly work our way out of this mess, but we would never stop planning. We heard the door click and was fixing to start pampering Sam when he miraculously sat up and talked normal. "What are you doing?" We asked in awe. "Shhh!!! I don't have too much time, but something is strange on this ship. For some reason they want to keep us here and I believe they have others." He said quickly. "What are you talking about little brother? What happened to that raspy voice?"

"I do have some bruised ribs, but I am basically feeling much better. I am faking most of the sickness because I feel like I can find out what is going on down here while you work on information up top. We must play this out and figure out how to get away safely." Where was the quiet, meek Sam that we had known our whole lives? The new Sam had taken initiative to be brave and in control of the situation not wait on Billy to tell him what to do. I liked this new Sam and we both agreed with his plan. We heard the click of the door and my next question was assured before I could ask. Mullet was back with a tray of food. It included fresh fruit, slices of meat, bread and water. They were at least taking care of him. We went along with his plot to pretend to stay sick. We pretended to wake him and force him to drink. "Sam, sit up and drink. The more you drink and eat, the stronger you will get." Billy said as he sat on the bed helping his brother. "Come on and sit up so I can help you drink." Mullet stepped up and moved both of us out of the way. "He can do it himself. The more he does on his own, the faster he will heal." Mullet growled at us. Even though we knew that Sam was much better than he was acting, I felt that I better make a little fuss so that Mullet wouldn't grow suspicious. "He's sick. It's going to take him some time to get his energy back enough to feed himself. Just let us help him a little." Then he snapped and ordered us to the door. He sat the tray close enough for Sam to get what he wanted, then opened the door and led us out. I couldn't help being worried about him because we didn't have any idea what they planned to do with or to us. One thing that gave me comfort was the thought that they were taking care of him and why would they do that if they were planning on hurting him. As we walked I heard a noise that gave me chill bumps. I stopped in my tracks to listen more closely. It was a crying sound. I wanted to listen longer but Billy was nudging me from behind. He was trying to tell me not to let Mullet know that we heard anything. We didn't want to draw suspicion where we wouldn't be allowed down here anymore. I knew that I had to get back down here soon. By the time we got back to the top deck, my stomach was cramping from hunger. Mullet wasn't as dumb as he looked so he offered us some food. We ate basically the same thing as Sam. I was engrossed in eating all that I could because we weren't sure when we would get to eat again. Ok, I couldn't eat as much as I thought because my stomach had shrunk over the past couple of weeks. I wasn't feeling so well and knew that I had eaten too quickly. I didn't eat another bite but knew that I had eaten enough to gain a little energy. They were feeding us well for some reason. They weren't cannibals, so I didn't think they were fattening us up to eat us, so what could it be? By this time, the sun was blazing and we were beginning to get anxious for what the day held. "What is going on?" I asked him. "I'm not real sure but it looks like work. They look very busy." He seemed to be saying but I wasn't paying much attention because I found myself staring at him. He had matured over the time we had been away from the village. However long that had been. His beautiful green eyes had narrowed to worried slants and his lips were full and red. I focused back on his voice and realized that he caught me staring at him. "Eleven days and ten nights." He said to me out of the blue. "Huh?" I stumbled. "We've been away for eleven days and ten nights." He explained. "How did you know what I was thinking?" Well that was part of what I was thinking and I wasn't about to tell him the other part. "I could just read it on your face. You are worried and I know that you are trying to be strong. Gosh, you have been strong, amazing actually." I looked away from him not sure what was going on and we had many other things to worry about right now. One of those things was right in front of us, shore. What were they going to do to us? We kept watching and allowed our eyes to focus more clearly on the activities ashore. They were digging, shoveling and moving dirt. "BLAST!" We immediately hit the deck. "What was that?" I asked as the rest of the men on the boat cheered in excitement. "Dynamite. They are blasting the hard dirt apart to make it easier to dig." Billy answered with a worried look on his face. What could be so important that they are blowing up the island? Are there really treasures buried on these islands? Or is it something else that they are searching for? I looked toward the back of the ship and noticed someone that I had not seen before. He was a tall, muscular built man observing the happenings with a pair of binoculars. He looked clean, I guess as clean as he could look considering he had been on the sea for a while. The men around him bustled about to ready another boat which was obviously his limo to shore. Mullet was behind us and started giving orders to the men. They had begun loading supplies such as bread, nuts, fruit, meat strips, and lots of digging tools. I recognized the shovels, but there were some tools that I was not familiar with. I looked over at Billy and knew his mind was turning with thoughts. Of what, I wasn't sure but I had a feeling it had something to do with escaping and what the heck were they looking for. We helped them fill bags with food and loaded them securely into the boat. When that task was finished, Billy pulled me out of the way. "Let's try to avoid them so that we don't have to go. 'Out of sight, out of mind' is the best strategy for us." We turned to walk to our hitching post, that's where they had us tied when we first arrived, sat down and started nibbling on some nuts. "Are you ready for another swim?" He asked me. "What? Are you considering swimming to shore?" I answered his question with a question. We had swam a lot farther so I knew we could do it. The question was how could we do it and not get caught? "Yes, I want to know what is going on and maybe be prepared if they decide to take us to shore. There is no way that we can get away until Sam is well enough to make the trip, so we may as well find out everything we can about these people and our surroundings. Let's go let Sam know what we are planning and then we will get going." We were already sneaking to the stairway that Mullet had led us through before. I wanted to snoop around and look for what made that crying sound that I had heard before, but I knew this was not the time. We went in the room and Sam seemed to be sound asleep and breathing heavily. I reached down and touched his hand trying not to scare him. He barely opened his eyes then jolted up out of bed. "We thought you had gotten really sick again. Why were you breathing so hard?" I said as I jumped back from him. "No, I am really healing quickly. I still act like I'm sick so that I can stay down here and snoop a little longer. I was out of bed when I heard someone coming, so I had to run back to bed." He explained to us. I was a little jealous that he got to stay in bed and be catered to while we were baking in the hot sun. We quickly explained what was going on and told him that we would fill him in on the details later. Before our luck ran out, we headed back to the deck to see the men had already loaded supplies into the small boats. He didn't have time to tell me the plan, so I just followed his lead. He grabbed two ropes and we climbed slowly over the railing and lowered ourselves in the water. He tied one rope to a boat and tossed me the other so that I could do the same. Finally, he spoke, "Try to stay on the side of the boat and be ready to hold your breath until they get completely loaded and start rowing to shore." I held the rope and stayed as close to the water as I could. It wasn't long until we saw the men climbing down the side to get in and go. As soon as they stepped in, we took deep breaths and went under. A few seconds passed and I felt myself being pulled. The men were strong enough to pull the boats at decent speeds, but I did have enough time to take quick breaths when I needed to. It wasn't too long before I could feel the bottom and knew that we were close to shore. I released some of the rope because I knew when we got to shore the men were sure to pull the boats up on land and then they were sure to see us. I could see the front of the boat cruise onto land and they didn't waste any time getting out and unloading the supplies. I let go of the rope and stayed under until their backs were turned. Billy grabbed my arm and motioned for me to come with him. We swam around to the left of the cove where there were no men working and coverage was available for us to hide. We crawled through the shallow water onto shore all the way to the lush green arms waiting to receive us. At last, we had reached a place where we could rest and watch. There were men everywhere and they were shoveling and sifting through the dirt. "Whatever they are looking for must be very valuable like gold, diamonds or some famous lost treasure. Look over at that pile. It has different looking rocks than the other piles. It looks like that group of men is cleaning the dirt off of each stone like they are looking for some long lost mysterious stone." He was giving me his view when we both gasped and we looked at each other. "The Green Stone!" Could it be? It wasn't like it was a huge diamond or anything; it was a green jewel like an emerald. Surely, they are not that valuable. I was running different ideas in my mind as we sat and watched for hours. They worked diligently and only stopped to eat one time. They were allowed to drink as much as they needed. I guess the man in charge was smart enough to know that he had to keep the men hydrated so that they could continue working. We noticed there was a change in pace and the men were putting some of their tools in a crude shed that they had obviously thrown together for that purpose. They loaded any leftover food and the small tools in their bags to take back to the ship. "Let's get back to the boats before they do or we could get left." I agreed and we crawled back to the water and swam quietly to the small boats. I held tightly to the rope and allowed it to pull me. By the time we got back and the men we busy doing their evening 'chores' we started unloading the supplies for them. As we crawled back onto the ship, Buzzard was waiting on us with an irritated look on his face. Buzzard was second in charge next to Mullet and had been assigned to keep an eye on us. I quickly looked at Billy as he simply held up the bags to explain to him where we had been. He fell for it and didn't even mention that we were soaking wet. Buzzard was lazier than the others and didn't really care what we were doing as long as he could tell Mullet that he knew where we were. He turned and walked away and I exhaled the air that was lodged in my lungs. We put the food away and sat by the hitching post and thought for awhile. I went over, grabbed some food and juice and came back to share with Billy. He ripped apart a piece of bread and handed me half. We continued to sit silently and chewed slowly on the bread. "I just can't understand what is going on, because they really don't pay us much attention and the captain hasn't even acknowledged us being on his ship." He said breaking the silence. "Yeah, just a few weeks ago we were swimming and being kids and then we were literally sucked into this nightmare. Have we sailed far from where we started? " I added. "I am not really sure, but this island does look similar to the one we were on. Now that I think about it, we may have just gone around the cove to the other side. Remember the first night we watched them fight? Well, since they caught us we have been anchored the whole time except briefly so hopefully we haven't gone too far." He got up and started walking around looking out at the island. Maybe he saw it differently than I had, because all islands looked basically the same to me. "Let's go check on Sam." We noticed that most of the crew was resting or had already retired for the night. The next shift was a small group of men that stood watch through the night. These men were not among the ones who had worked the whole day on the island so they were fresh and ready for any intruders. They didn't seem too worried about us so it was pretty easy to slip away to the lower deck at this moment. We found him sitting up in bed. "Hey you look better." I said. "Yeah, you know that I have sort of been faking it. I did feel really bad at first, but all of a sudden I began to heal miraculously. I keep faking my illness so that I can snoop around down here." Sam told us. "So what have you found? You can't do this much longer because we can't get away as long as you are down here." Billy said in a harsh tone, "Well, I am not sure what they are up to but I really don't think it includes us. I think we actually came upon them and now they don't know what to do with us." Sam ignored his brother's tone. "You know, you could be right. What about your leg? The infection was horrible when we got here." I tried to break in the conversation to give Billy time to calm down. "You won't believe it!" He said as he pulled the blanket back and we stared with our mouths open. "It's a miracle! How can it be?" We almost yelled. The puss infected gashes were gone. There was no evidence of a scar or wound. We were baffled and then a worried look came on Billy's face. "How are you going to get away with this any longer without a wound?"

"I have been changing the wound myself before they come to check on me." He explained. Before we could respond, he began telling us about another kid on board. He was about our age and very sick. "O my gosh, that was the moaning sound I heard the first time we came down here to see you. Does anyone else know that you know about the kid?"

"No, he doesn't know anything yet, but he is suspicious of my illness so I have to get as much information as soon as possible. I will do the best that I can until they send me up to the deck to work. I just have to find a way to stay down here and help the kid." He told us. "We have to come up with a plan either way. We cannot stay on this ship forever even for some kid. We will include him in our plans to escape if he is well enough to move." As Billy said this I watched him sit in deep thought before I said, "What? What are you thinking?"

"It just doesn't make sense. Why would there be another kid on board? We ended up here because we explored that underwater cave that sucked us through to another world. But where did he come from? Have you been able to talk to him?" He said. Sam replied by saying, "I don't know anything about him, but I am going to find out."

"Hey!" A loud voice boomed from the door. Buzzard was coming through before we could say another word. "Get out of here and get on deck. There is work to be done before bedtime." We jumped up and followed his command and I heard Billy whisper to Sam, "Be careful while prowling around the ship. We don't know these men, but we have seen first hand how dangerous they can be." We headed back up to the deck to find Buzzard a good bit irritated with us, so we went straight over to him to find out what work he intended us to do. We started peeling some weird fruit and cracking coconuts. I took over the peeling while Billy started hammering a sharp tool down into the coconut. I looked up from my work and noticed the men who had been casually walking the deck were suddenly bustling about like there was some emergency on board. As soon as I noticed how busy it was, it stopped just as fast. They all moved to the side of the ship and looked very nervous. I allowed my eyes to follow down the line until they reached the center of the ship, the captain. The same big, distinguished looking man that had appeared earlier was once again leering at everyone. He looked dangerous and after staring at him for a minute or two I realized his dark eyes were staring a hole straight through me. I didn't know what to do, so I slowly let my eyes drift down to the fruit in my lap. "Wonder what that was all about?" Billy asked. "I don't know, but I do know that it made me feel very uneasy." I answered. Then, suddenly he was standing above us. To be more exact, he was directly above me. I stared at the toe of his boots and slowly worked my eyes up to meet his. Just like I thought he was staring straight down at me. "Get up." He ordered in the scariest voice I had ever heard. I laid down the fruit and stood. I had always considered myself tall for a girl, but I was minute compared to the captain of this ship. "You will come ashore and help us dig tomorrow, both of you. You had to put your noses in our business, so now you will work like the rest of the crew on this ship." He growled. I could smell his horrid breath and I am sure that he could smell the fear easing its way out of my skin. I couldn't speak at the moment so I just nodded to let him know that I understood his orders. He turned and left the deck and it seemed everyone exhaled the breath that we were all holding in our lungs. We went back to our duties which took us until the sun went down. We had food abundantly that night, not just fruit and coconut but a very tasty meat and bread. It was like a special holiday treat. I ate my share and pondered the events around me. Was this real or some horrible dream? Were we thrown back in time? I didn't think so because they didn't look like the pirates in the movies with eye patches, peg legs and parrots. Yes, they were dirty and stinky but they looked like just bad men up to no good. That's it! They were robbers of the seas, capturing cargo ships that were just unlucky and passed over the wrong waters. I knew they had to be searching for something, too, because they had been digging on that island and we would be joining them in the morning. We were taken to our rooms which were actually clean little rooms with a bed, dresser and small bathroom to the side. I quickly showered and fell asleep with many thoughts running through my head. I tossed and turned all night with the memories of the last few days leaving me with a sense that I have missed something. I can figure this out. I just need a little more information in my dreams. It always works the same way where I am dreaming and get so close to the answers that I need and then I am suddenly jolted awake. This time, it is a pounding at the door that is so hard that I can almost hear my heartbeat. It was pounding so hard that I could barely breathe. I dressed quickly and headed to the deck just as the sun was showing itself on the horizon. It was an amazing sight. The big yellow ball was surrounded by this blast of oranges and reds. One side of this could be an incredible trip watching the sunset and the animals come alive with the day. I stood watching the mothers waking, feeding and cleaning their babies. It seemed that no matter the species, most mothers shared some of the same habits when caring for their young. Mothers, I haven't even thought of my own mother in a few days, because we had been so busy and trying to survive. I realized how much I missed her and I had to fight back tears which fought their way to the surface anyway. I wasn't too successful in hiding my feelings when it came to her. I wiped the tears away and began helping the others load the boats with food and more tools. It was going to be a long, hot day unless by chance we found whatever they were eagerly searching for. I climbed down the side of the ship into one of the boats and began paddling along side of Billy. The men really didn't need our help but we wanted to pull our own weight and seem needed. We reached the island and unloaded the supplies. The men went straight to work in different directions knowing exactly what to do without asking or being told. Some began chopping wood for a fire while others filled buckets of water. "Come with me, you two will help us dig." Billy and I each took a shovel and followed them to the grounds that were being invaded. We dug and dug while the others sifted through the sand. When we obviously it water, we were told to keep digging. "Are you really expecting to find some ancient treasure that was buried hundreds of years ago?" Billy asked sarcastically. The man just growled at him and kept working. Our work was interrupted by hoops and hollers from another site and everyone's attention was set on them. The captain made his way over to see what all the excitement was about. The men handed him their little treasure. We eased closer to see that it was chunks of gold, real gold from the earth. The captain seemed fairly excited but that obviously wasn't what he was looking for. "Dig, it has to be here. This was the last place she was seen alive and this was where I put her." As the captain told his men, Billy and I gasped at what we thought he meant. I didn't even inquire, but looked down to see my hands were bleeding and making new blisters on top of blisters. I was hoping the gold would end the dig at least for the day. As I was trying to forget about the sense of touch, one of my other senses kicked in and my nose smelled food. I had to rest because my whole body was aching. I sat down and looked out onto the horizon, not thinking, just looking. I didn't even realize Billy was trying to hand me a container of water until he placed it in my hands. I let my hand gently grip it and began drinking until I felt my stomach get sick. Billy reached over and grabbed the water and noticed my hands. "Charli, your hands are bleeding!" He said with a combination of sadness and anger. "I know but they are just hands and I will be fine." I tried to convince him. "No, you are not fine. We have to get away from here and I don't care what Sam is up to. We are not going to be out here working everyday while he is up in bed being pampered. We can't risk our lives and our escape for some kid that we don't even know. They haven't put their hands on us to hurt us, but I know that you are hurting all over your body. Let's get Sam tonight and leave." He was talking so fast that I only concentrated on his last statement. "Where would we go, Billy? I am scared and I am not sure if the 'unknown' is not worse than this." I said as I tried to keep my voice from breaking. "Are you crazy? I can take care of us and there is plenty to eat on the island. We can do it." Billy was determined to get us out of there and I knew that I was relying on him to do it. The captain broke our conversation when he called us to eat. We walked down to the fire and were served a bowl of some kind of stew. I was so hungry that I didn't even care what was in the bowl and I didn't have the energy to complain. After gulping down the first bowl, I wasn't feeling so well. I walked down to the water and washed out my bowl. I took a few extra minutes to wash my face in hopes of feeling better. It didn't help too much so I just walked over to Billy as he said, "I will do the digging and you help them sift."

"Ok, but what I am I looking for if not for gold?" I asked knowing that he had also noticed the captain's reaction earlier when they showed him the chunks. "I'm not sure but it must be something special." We made our way back to our digging spot and Billy began to dig immediately. He dug for the rest of the day until it was time to load back into the boats and paddle back to the ship. For the first time since we had been here, I noticed how beautiful the ship really was. The wood looked like something in an expensive antique store. It was well taken care of and obviously handled the sea. I was still admiring the beauty of this magnificent beast when I realized I had already climbed aboard. I went straight below deck to my room before anyone could give me orders. I quickly jumped in the shower, put on the pajamas that were given to everyone, and slipped into bed. I lay there on the single bed and fell into the same annoying dream as before. I didn't want to dream because I thought too much. I just wanted to sleep soundly for once. It didn't happen. My conscience was trying to tell me some answers about what was going on but I just couldn't figure it out. "Mmmm, ohhh, mmmm!" I fought coming out of my sleep, but the moaning sounds were getting louder and louder. I was awake, dead still, and listening. I slowly sat up wondering what it could be then stepped to the floor. I tip-toed to the door and had to stop for a second to control my breathing. I turned the knob and quietly stepped into the hall. I wasn't sure what time it was, but I knew it was in the middle of the night because I could hear snoring. There were three different snores going on at the same time, but I welcomed the noise because they covered the sound of my feet. The ship was just as beautiful below deck with its deep antique wood and lanterns. At the same time this beauty bestowed an eerie feeling as I eased my way down the dark hall. The captain of this ship matched its structure by his huge frame, distinguished walk, and deep eerie voice. He seemed to be cleaner than what I imagined sailors to be, but I knew he was not one to fool around with. We just stayed away from him and did what we were told. I got my mind back to the task at hand and that was finding the source of the moan. The farther I walked the closer I was getting to the sound. I knew Sam had told us that there was a kid on board, but my curiosity led me to search for myself. I eased my way down the hall until I heard the moan coming from behind a door. "Huh!" My heart lunged up in my throat just as a large hand clasped my shoulder. It was him, the captain looking down at me with black cold eyes. "I, I, I was looking for Sam. I have been worried about him and didn't get a chance to check on him today." I stuttered. I was so scared. Before I could say anything else he said in a cold deep voice, "You don't move about my ship without my permission and your friend is down that way." He pointed in the opposite direction. "Next time you want to see him you will request to be taken to him. Do you understand?" He leaned a little closer waiting for an answer. "Yes, sssir." I stammered. Then he placed both hands on my shoulders, turned me around, and gave me a light shove. I went back to my room and before closing the door I took a chance and peeked out to see the huge silhouette standing in the hall watching my every move. I backed into my room and crawled back into bed. I lay there awhile thinking of home and couldn't get Madame Scary out of my thoughts. She seemed to know about the secrets of the cave and she acted like she was genuinely worried about us. With those last thoughts, sleep finally came. I slept hard with no dreams and no moving around. Before I knew what was happening, it was once again time to dig. I felt better than I did the day before but was still a little sore. I tried to eat as much fruit for breakfast without getting sick. I didn't want to dehydrate or make Billy do all the work when I knew that we had a lot ahead of us. From the small boats to shore none of us spoke. I guess we weren't the only ones that were exhausted because everyone seemed to drag a little this morning. Billy and I made eye contact and I tried to smile because he was looking at me with great concern. We walked back to our dig site and got busy. Today, we were given gloves which helped tremendously. We took turns digging and sifting through the sand. I knew that he took longer shifts digging, but I didn't have the energy to complain. I just couldn't keep up with him. This same routine continued for four more days until we heard someone yell after about two hours into our work. "We have something! Come over and look, Captain." Many of the crew members hurried over to look being careful not to get in front of their beloved captain. They stood looking into what looked like a freshly dug grave. Grave? For some reason that thought or picture gave me goose bumps. "Is that what we have been digging for all this time?" I whispered to Billy. "That's what it looks like from here. Come on, let's ease closer and get a better look." He said as he crept closer to the hole. Before we could get close enough to actually see down in there, the captain jumped down on something that made a thump. Oh, no the only thing that it could be is a coffin. I felt a lump in my throat, but couldn't make myself look away. It was like a reward for all this work. I looked over at Billy and he was motioning me to get down. I wasn't sure what he meant, but I just followed his lead. He was on all fours crawling through them until he reached the edge of the hole. I wasn't sure that I wanted to be this close to whatever was fixing to be revealed but again I couldn't resist. We leaned in as far as we could and saw the captain prying open a wooden box, a body box. The wood began to crack and splinter when suddenly it opened. I couldn't see anything at first because instinctively I shut my eyes. Suddenly, an angry shout came from the captain and the onlookers took a few quick steps backwards. I continued to stare at the box. Empty, it was empty. I looked up and heard the captain yelling, "Where is she? Where is the hag? She was dead! I saw her die. She was put in that box and buried right here! Where is she? How can this be?" This is exactly the rage that I had feared was inside the giant leader of this crew. He was still yelling as he stomped across the sand, entered one of the boats, and headed back to his ship. "I don't know what this means, but I hope it means we don't have to dig anymore." Billy explained. There was lots of hush mumbling around us, but we couldn't make out their words. We gathered up tools and headed back. Thank goodness, a short workday was one good thing that came out of this day. When we climbed aboard we felt the tension and nervousness of the crew. It was silent, too silent. We headed straight to our rooms, but I decided to follow Billy to his. "What was that about?" I asked. I was too wound up to rest so I started asking him questions. "Obviously, he has killed someone and expected to find the body. Who? Why? What does he need a dead body for?" He answered me bluntly. "It must be important because they have been searching a long time before we got here because there were many fresh dig sites." He stopped to think, then said, "I knew we were looking for gems like some type of lost treasure, but why a body? What could a body have that he would want? He said that he put it there so why doesn't he know what is on it? Also, didn't he say it was a she?" I just nodded at all his questions and listened quietly. "Maybe it was his wife or some relative. Did he actually kill her or did he get someone else to do it?" I didn't answer I just shivered with the thoughts. We both sat with the events of the day going through our brains. "Let's go see Sam." He said. "Well, we have to request a visit from now on." When he looked at me funny I continued telling him about the captain catching me snooping around the night before. "Are you crazy? He could have hurt you." He scolded. "I told him that I wanted to check on Sam because we didn't get a chance to see him and he seemed to believe me."

"Well, you may not be so lucky next time." He scolded again. "I know, but let's get permission and go see Sam." I said trying to change the subject. We went to the top deck and found Mullet. We requested a visit and Mullet led the way. Since we had built trust with him he dropped us off with Sam as he went to take care of his own business. Sam was still faking his illness until he realized that it was us. "Hey guys! Come closer because we don't want anyone to hear us. I got into the boy's room and he was very ill with a high fever and hallucinating." He began telling us. "Wait, what do you mean was? Did he die? Did they kill him?" I said in a panicked tone. "Shhh…" Sam snapped at me. "No, Charli. What I mean is that he has healed. I have spent the last couple of days with him and he has completely healed. He has no fever, nothing." Billy and I just stared at him as he continued. "I don't know how to explain it, but he was dying two days ago like he was having a hard time breathing and within an hour of my visit he started getting better." We were still staring at him when Billy broke the silence. "What now? We can't stay here forever. We must start planning on how to get off this ship and back to the village." The village, just hearing that made me wonder how long we had been missing. I hadn't forgotten home, but not thinking about it sure made it a little easier. I was brought out of my trance when Billy reached over and touched me. That's when I felt the warm tear make its way down my cheek. "It will be okay, Charli. We will find a way to get home. If we are patient, we will come up with a plan that will work." He assured me. "I know. I have just tried not to think about it for awhile because I can't see how we can get away, especially now that we have seen and heard so much." I cried. "Patience, we have to be patient and we will do it." Right now I really wanted to believe every word that he said, so I nodded and tried to smile as he pulled me into his arms. To change the subject, Billy told Sam about what happened at the dig site. "Yeah, we found a coffin, a wooden coffin." Sam asked what was in it with a slight flicker of excitement in his voice. "Nothing. That is what made the captain so angry. He was expecting a body, a female body that he claimed to have put in there himself. We don't have time to figure it out because we have to worry about our own plans. I think we need to make our escape at night even though it will be dangerous. We have to spend some time studying our location and what everything looks like. Hopefully, that will keep us from getting lost and we will be able to find our way back to the cliff." We both agreed with him, but Sam looked upset. "What is it, Sam?" I asked. I was just thinking of the kid down the hall. We can't just leave him here. He has to go with us. He isn't sure how he got here because he just woke up and was inside of his cabin. He has never left the cabin so he doesn't know anything about the rest of the ship. He should be well enough to travel, but I want him to continue to fake it so that we can stay below deck." Sam pleaded for us to take the kid. "Well I hope you are enjoying yourself down here resting while Charli and I have been working from sun up to sun down. Just look at her hands." He snatched my hand out of my lap and flipped it over for him to see. The blisters were exposed and my finger tips were raw meat. We were also burned miserably from the sun. I couldn't help but feel sorry for Sam when he looked down at my hands and quickly looked up at me and said in a little boy voice, "Sorry."

"It is fine, Sam. Don't worry about it. Let's just work on getting out soon before the captain decides to leave the island and we never get back home." I tried to comfort the little boy in front of me. Even though he was only two years younger than me he seemed much more immature sometimes. I knew Billy was still irritated with him, but he finally agreed that we had much more important things to worry about. We made our way to the hall and waited for Mullet to come back to get us. We knew how to get back to our rooms, but we didn't want to break his trust. A few minutes passed and Mullet walked past us and said, "Get to your rooms." He left us there without even checking to see if we had followed his orders. We did. I entered my room, said goodnight to Billy and shut the door. I sat on the edge of the bed and just rested my brain. Before I let self pity take over and tears build, I went to the bathroom and took a long shower. The next morning no one came to wake us so I took advantage of the extra time to sleep. I dreamed. I was home with my family and life was normal in the village. Sam, Billy and I had plans to go down to the beach so I was gathering my gear and she appeared. Madame Scary was looking at me and mouthing something. I was startled at first and at the same time I desperately wanted to know what she was trying to tell me. For some reason I wasn't afraid of her. There was a difference in her expression that comforted me. What? I focused in on her mouth and what she was saying. "Run! G…" I made out some at first, but I needed her to tell me so I screamed it in my dream. "Run! Gooooo to the green claw! Now!" She mouthed to me. Suddenly a rush of air charged down my throat to my lungs and I sat straight up in bed. What was that about? I questioned my sanity. What did she mean when she said the green claw? I have to tell Billy I decided. I jumped out of bed, brushed my teeth, and went straight to his room. I didn't even care about getting caught because I needed to tell him right now. As I reached his room, he opened the door and stood there with this desperate look on his face. At the same time, we said, "green claw." I looked at him confused wondering how he knew what I was going to say. Understanding my confusion, he started explaining his dream which was the same dream that I had just awakened from. "How, how could this happen? How could we have the same dream?" I asked him. "I don't know but I thought it was a nightmare until just now." I didn't because I had been having them for some time. "I know, but did you see the look on her face? She looked sincere like she was really trying to help us." I reminded him. "We have to figure this out soon. We have to find the green claw and what it means and we have to start looking now." I noticed how he put stress on the word now, just like Ms. Byrtle did in my dream. "Charli, something is going on with the crew. They are making plans because no one came down to get us. I think they're moving and if we don't get away now, we may never get away." Reality set in with his words and I knew he was right. We had to run now! "Okay, what do we do?" I asked. "First, you go round up a few necessities for us and I will go tell Sam. Meet me back here in thirty minutes. We will have to figure out what or where the claw is." His plan sounded like a good start and I am sure that he would have the next step figured out when we met back. We took off in separate directions. I didn't have a lot of time because I had not planned on taking this lovely last minute vacation. I was trying to make light of the situation because I knew that I was nervous about this move. The first thing that I grabbed was the left over medicine that I got from Ms. Byrtle. Water, we need water. I grabbed some waters and snacks that I had hidden under my cot, and then looked around the room to find something to carry the supplies in safely. The only thing that would even come close to working was my pillow case. Well, it would have to do because the room was basically empty except for the bare necessities. I grabbed the pillow case full of supplies and went out the door to Billy's room. "So, what did Sam say?" I asked as soon as I walked in the room. "He is getting his things and going to tell that kid down the hall. I explained to him that if he wasn't well enough that we would have to leave him and Sam got all upset. I told him that we could not risk all of us for this kid that we don't even know." As Billy rambled on, I found myself just staring at him again. I was amazed that he was suddenly so mature and something else that I wasn't ready to admit. I quickly looked away and tried to concentrate on our situation. "Let's get to the top deck and start trying to figure out the message that Ms. Byrtle is trying to tell us." He said. "Okay." I said and followed Billy with the same weird feelings. The other men were busy working, but their leader and a few others were in serious conversation away from us. "Just act as normal as possible and look around the ship. They know that we realize something is different, so we don't have to hide that. We just need to go with the flow of the atmosphere of everyone else." I nodded and turned to walk around the ship looking out on the horizon. What am I looking for? A green claw? How can a claw be green? What kind of claw? Is it a cat claw? No, not living on the sea. Hmm? Oh, oh, a crab claw. That had to be it. This all started with a crab claw, but what could that tell us? "Billy, could we be looking for a crab claw? "Yes, that is it, Charli! Oh my, what does that mean? What is a green crab claw? Green cl…aw? I got it, Charli. The stone that we found was in a crab claw, but how is that going to help us get away? And why did she tell us to run to it? I stood for a long time trying to figure out the mysterious message until Billy got up and left. A few minutes later he was back. He looked very nervous. "What's wrong? Is everything alright?" I suddenly got nervous too. "Yeah, everything is fine for now, but we do have to be very careful. I got the stone from Sam." Before he said anything else I realized that I was holding my breath. Just the sight of that stone took my breath away. It was mesmerizing. "The stone is the key to getting away so we have to figure out how to use it. Keep watch because we can't let anyone see the stone." He told me and I immediately began to watch. The men were actually very busy securing everything on deck and making sure the small boats were also secured to the sides of the ship. We were leaving. Oh no, we didn't have much time left because they were working diligently to complete their tasks. I turned to see Billy looking through the green stone like it was a telescope. He was looking out toward the island. "Oh my gosh! Charli, I see it. I see the green claw that Ms. Byrtle was telling us about. If you look through the stone you will see a huge cliff coming up out of the north side of the island." I looked and couldn't see anything then he slipped the green stone in my hand. "I'll keep watch and you look through it." He told me. "Ahhh," was all that I could manage to get out. It was just as he said. When I looked through the stone a great cliff appeared and the top was shaped like a giant crab claw. With the stone, it was a giant green crab claw. "We have to get away tonight. That will give us a head start. At dark, be ready to swim." As I handed him the stone, I found myself staring into his green eyes that I had not really noticed before this exploration that we were on right now. They weren't deep green like the stone, but crystal clear green like the sea. What? What is wrong with me? Yuk! I couldn't think about Billy that way, he was my best friend. We stood for a little longer staring out at the ocean, island and at the men bustling about the deck. We didn't dare take out the stone again. We knew what we had to do. It was settled. No matter what we were running away tonight. I walked over and grabbed a few pieces of fruit and dried meat and stashed them for later. I nibbled on a piece of the meat just in case someone saw me grab some food. We didn't need anyone getting suspicious now. I turned to go to my room and saw Billy doing the same thing. We knew that we had a long journey ahead of us so we had to be prepared. It was real! We were actually taking off and we had no idea what would happen to us if they caught us. Would they hurt us? Would they kill us? We didn't know, but we had seen them kill other men on the ships they had raided so we had to make sure that our plan was going to work. I went straight to my room and added the supplies to my pillowcase. I cut some slits in the top of the case and weaved a string through it to make it like a drawstring. I pulled it tight and put my arms through like it was a crude little back pack. I thought that I was ready to go and realized the sun was actually setting faster than I wanted it to. I was excited about going home, but there were many dangers to be faced on the way. We weren't stupid and we knew this was not going to be easy. I felt a little nauseous and my stomach was working like a roller coaster. My stomach was flying up in my throat then dropping rapidly to my toes. My door slowly cracked open and the boys walked in quietly. "It's almost time to go. The deck is clear and everyone is settled in their rooms. You and I are going to load our packs in the smallest boat, get it untied and lowered. Sam and the kid will meet us." Billy began. "I am ready." I stammered. Billy hesitated for a brief moment and we made eye contact. "We can do it, Charli. I promise." I didn't answer. I just checked my pack and followed him quietly out the door and to the top deck. I just needed to be busy and try not to think about the plan ahead. I helped Billy untie the boat and we lowered it into the water. We slipped over the side of the boat and climbed down and got settled in while we waited on Sam and the kid. I couldn't look up at Billy because I hated showing weakness, and I knew that he would read it all over my face. My thoughts were interrupted when the other two were sneaking over the railing and slithering down into the boat. The kid had no problem at all getting down the rope, but Sam struggled with the task. Finally, we were all in and automatically began rowing. We rowed in time with each other to keep the boat straight toward shore. I knew we had time to get to shore but we had no idea how to get to the giant green claw. Rowing to shore seemed easy enough probably because our adrenaline was pumping. We jumped out of the boat as Billy dragged it up into the woods. It was darker in the woods because the trees blocked the moon from providing us with any light. Our eyes strained to focus in the darkness which at least helped us see one another. Run, that is all my brain could register. I had never been this scared in all my life. The green monster of jungle engulfed us. It wrapped its huge arms around us and slapped us all over our faces, arms, and legs at the same time. It breathed its hot, steamy breath down on us as we struggled to get away. I guess Billy felt that we had a good head start because he suddenly stopped running and we all collapsed beside him. My chest heaved up and down and my heart pumped blood so fast that my chest was burning. Billy spoke to us, "Everyone drink a little and take a few bites for energy. We will only rest for a short while then we will go again. No one said a word but we all followed his orders. The time passed quickly as we took a few more sips of water. We began walking quickly through the thick maze. "We need to cover as much ground as possible and then we will try to rest. When we have a good enough lead on them we will actually lie down for a while." Again we followed Billy's instructions. It was natural how we had matured and taken on roles without being assigned. Billy was obviously in charge, Sam was taken care of the new kid and I became the nurturer and provider. I made sure everyone drank and ate just enough but not too much. We kept a steady pace throughout the night until the kid collapsed holding his stomach. He was wailing as he rocked back and forth then he started gagging. "What's wrong? Are you cramping up from running or do you feel sick?" Sam asked in a panicked voice. At this time, we had not even heard him talk at all. "I don't know, but I can't run anymore. I am hurting all over." He cried with the same strange accent as most of the crew members. "Sam, we can't stop yet, we will have to help carry him." Billy firmly stated. "No, I can't go any further. I can't do it." He continued to cry. "You will let us carry you or you will be left behind. We will not be caught like this." Billy's voice had suddenly grown louder and with more force. "Now get up and let's go." He commanded. Sam grabbed one arm and Billy grabbed the other and they assisted the kid as we moved as quickly as we could. I continued to carry the supplies and led the way for the boys. We walked for at least a few more hours then Billy stopped. "Let's get some rest here in this clearing." I was already unpacking enough food and water for us to regain some of our strength. I was exhausted and sat for a second to get my thoughts together when I felt someone push my hair out of my face. I looked up to make eye contact with Billy. We had grown up together and had spent almost every day of our lives together, but now the connection was different. I knew what that look meant to me, but I didn't know what it meant to him. "Charli, how much water do we have?" He asked. "We should have plenty if we are careful with it. We can also drink the juice from the fruit that I brought or find some out here. I have been trying to make sure that we all have the same amount." I answered. With that he offered to give the kid his share this time and I told him, "No, we need you to be the strongest to get us through this. We have enough if we all do as I say. Trust me, please." I begged. He gave in and gave me the sweetest smile like he was proud of me. I needed that smile right now because I was so tired and sore. The smile made red heat rise up my neck to my cheeks so I turned away and started rationing out some food for our dinner. It wasn't a full course meal, but it was sufficient. We gathered some soft leaves for bedding and we laid down to rest. I didn't dream this time I actually slept. I slept too well. How could I sleep when we were in the middle of who knows where being sought out by crazy people? Suddenly I realized why I was so relaxed. My head was on Billy's chest. I slowly rolled away from him and sat up. I got enough food and water for us all and noticed the kid was not here. I turned around to see Billy looking at me and noticed something was wrong. Before he could ask me I said, "He is gone." He shot to his feet when we both saw the kid coming toward us. "Where have you been?" He snapped. "I had to crap. Those stomach cramps turned in to diarrhea." He whimpered. "Well, you should let someone know when you leave again. I don't care what the reason is." Billy moved toward him to show that he was serious. The kid nodded and we began packing our supplies. It was almost daylight and I was getting more worried about the men, even though there was no way we could get caught now. Still, we ran. I felt sweat burning the new cuts on my legs and arms. My lungs were drawing in air like a giant air balloon that had enough to reach the moon. We began to slow at the next clearing. We made sure that we had enough coverage to stay hidden, but found a place to sit and take a few sips. Billy took the green stone and looked for the cliff that took on the shape of a giant crab claw. The rest of us took this time to rest and snack. "We have to be rested enough because this will be our last time to stop if we are going to make it there by dark. That's our ruby slippers, our way home." He said. "Yeah, but what do we do when we get to the cliff?" Sam asked. "Well, the green stone is leading us so I assume it will get us the rest of the way. That's our only hope and we must trust that it will work." He tried to answer positively as we nibbled on some nuts and dried meat. I thought about what he said and whether it was right or wrong, it was our only hope. The green stone that Sam had found lodged in a crab's claw. What was so special about it? We didn't know, but we believed in it anyway. We believed in it because it was all that we had. We spent the rest of the day talking and resting. We walked some then rested and ate. We were so far ahead of the men that we didn't feel we had too much to worry about. My heart jumped in my throat with just the thought of them catching us. We couldn't be sure or get too comfortable. They were grown men and dangerous. "Charli, are you feeling well?" I jumped at his voice. I was in deep thought and he broke that silence with his words. "Billy, I am fine. I am just trying to keep the plan straight in my head."

"You need to rest while you can, or we can wait until later to start again." He suggested. "No, we are not wasting any time. I am fine and I can make it tonight." I let him know in a voice that reminded him that I was as tough as anyone else here. He walked away and tears tried to form in my eyes, but I quickly fought them back. I couldn't let them surface and ruin my tough image. I was not going to cry! Without realizing it, we had reached the other end of the island and standing straight in front of us was a giant cliff. As our eyes made their way up the cliff, we noticed that it looked like a giant crab claw was jutting out from the top. All four of us stopped dead in our tracks. The cliff glistened like a million flex of gold. It was breathtakingly beautiful. I couldn't help but wonder how we could not see this golden giant from across the sea, from the ship, from anywhere. "We have to swim to the claw for some reason that is where the stone has led us. That is also where Ms. Byrtle told us to go." Billy said aloud and Sam looked at him confused. "Let's take a break and fill our bodies with whatever is left so that we have enough strength to make this long swim ahead of us. We will take our time swimming because we can't swim real hard then stop to take a nap. We won't have the jungle to lie down in after we get started. We will have to pace ourselves." As he said this, I was already unpacking the food and separating it in four ways. I knew the three of us could make the swim, but I wasn't sure about the kid. I looked at him and noticed he was very fidgety. "Are you alright?" I asked and he just nodded. He looked to be about 13 or 14 but we knew nothing about him, and he didn't seem to want to offer any information. Where did he come from and how did he get on that ship? Did he just get unlucky like us? Did he lose his family in the process? He must not have any family because he was more than willing to go home with us. Then what? What would happen to him then? That was my last thought before I drifted off to sleep. I didn't sleep soundly, but was very restless. Something just didn't seem right. I couldn't figure out the reason for these dreadful feelings, but I knew that it wasn't good. I had to stop worrying. In the early morning, we would be swimming to the giant cliff that led to our homes. I was worrying for nothing. We were almost there and had gained enough lead on the crew that we didn't feel the need to be concerned. I felt myself fall into a deeper sleep and had no dreams. Then that familiar morning feeling awakened me. I had to go to the bathroom so I slipped away without waking the boys and took care of business. Man, the sun was already up and peeking at me through the leaves. It almost blinded me each time my eyes connected with a slither that made it through the lush of green. Something didn't look normal about the sun. Yes, it should be up, but not that bright. That's when I realized that it wasn't actually the sun, but it was the sun reflecting off of something. That couldn't be possible is what my brain was screaming at me, but my eyes were telling me something different. I pulled up my shorts quickly and moved closer to the strange light. "Oh, no!" I caught myself before he could hear me and went back to where the boys were still sleeping. I woke them quietly. "Billy, Billy wake up! O my gosh, wake up!" I whispered. "What is it?" He asked still in a disoriented state. He too had been sound asleep. "The kid is using something to reflect the sun. I think that he is trying to signal the ship." I told them. "He is doing what?" He asked as he jumped to his feet and trotted toward the kid. "Hey, what do you think you are doing? Why are you giving us up? Do you realize how dangerous those men are? Our first night out here we saw them execute some men on another ship. Do you want that to happen to us?" He was almost yelling at the kid. Billy reached him and continued yelling and shaking him. That is when the boy said something that made us all want to puke, "I am with them, you idiot! The captain is my father and your brother has something that we want, we need." He snapped back. "You piece of crap. Sam took care of you and you betrayed him, you betrayed all of us." He was about to punch him when I yelled at Billy, "Look, they saw the signal. They may be a good ways from us but we have to get out of here now. They will be coming shortly." He snatched up the kid and we ran back into the jungle out of view. We dumped everything out of the pillowcase, and Sam started tearing it into strips. We tied the kid as tight as possible. We didn't have time to question him, even though there was so much we wanted to know, or needed to know. "Let's go, it's the time we have been waiting for. It's time to go home." He grabbed my hand and led me to the beach with Sam following behind us. We ran to the water and went straight in, then noticed that Sam had not entered the water. "Sam, come on!" Billy scolded. I knew why he hadn't entered the water. He was remembering the attack by the creature that had left him deathly ill. "Sam, you have to come. It is the only way home." I walked back and gently took his hand. I noticed a tear in his eye and led him carefully through the water to Billy. We put him in between us and Billy turned to swim. I gently pushed Sam to get him going as we cruised through the water. We were halfway to the cliff when we heard the kid yelling obscenities at us. We turned and saw him jumping up and down. "We will catch you. There is no way you can get away from us now. Haaaahaaaa!" His voice and laughter had an eerie sound that just drove us to swim faster. He was right. The men were closing in on us and we couldn't waste a moment. "We will get that stone! We will have it!" As he yelled that we did stop for a moment to look at each other and back at him. "Yes, the stone, the green stone is what we want. We will find all the treasures in the world with that stone. It will lead you to your hearts desires. Didn't it lead you to yours? Didn't it lead you to this cliff which will lead you to your pitiful little homes?" As he babbled on we couldn't help but stare at him with stupid looks on our faces. "Come on, we don't have time to figure out what he is talking about. We have to beat them to the cliff." As we turned and faced the cliff we noticed that it was just a flat straight wall with no way to escape. We couldn't turn back so we just kept swimming. That cliff looked better than the alternative behind us and we had to have faith that we would find another underwater cave. We glanced back to see the kid working the sun's reflection so that the men could get to us. We continued swimming as fast as we could. We were so close to the cliff and I focused my eyes to a dark spot that appeared on the side of it. It looked similar to the cave that was the beginning of this whole journey. At this point the cave wasn't underwater, so we wouldn't be sucked in like before. It was probably too high for any of us to reach. "When we get there, Sam, be ready for us to boost you up to the ledge of the cave." When I thought that this was getting a little better, I saw movement in the dark cave. "There is something or someone in the cave. I just saw movement." I yelled at the boys. We weren't worried about being quiet because we knew the men could see us. I looked over and saw the horrible fear on Sam's face. "Not in the water, Sam. It was in the cave and it was probably a shadow where the waves are crashing against the walls of the cliff." Billy said as he moved ahead of us. I knew that he was trying to convince Sam that it was nothing to be afraid of, but I also knew that he saw it too. "Swim, faster they are coming around the last curve of the island." He demanded. We didn't even look back. We swam. Billy reached the cliff first and was already searching for a way for us to lift ourselves up in to the opening of the dark cave. We could barely hear the kid still yelling at us, but we were aware that he was. Finally, we made it and Billy and I each grabbed one of Sam's feet and gave him a boost. The first try was not high enough so we took a deep breath and went under water to push him up with all our strength. This time it was better, but I swallowed half of the salty sea as I was coming up for air. With the salt, I sucked air into my lungs and continued pushing him above my head. I watched his every move as our eyes made contact and we knew that we had to make this work. Billy nodded at me to assure me that we could do it. One more push with all my might would have to do the job. We took one last breath, went down, and kicked hard against the water. Sam was reaching for the ledge of the cave when a hand reached down and grabbed him. He was gone. "Sam!" We both screamed. "Oh no, Sam. Sam!" We called for him. At the same time, I felt a sharp pain at the back of my head. Billy had the fierce look of a wild dog ready to attack and he was coming toward me. He grabbed me and tried to pull me to him and the pain sharpened at the back of my head. I knew the men had reached us and one of them was trying to pull me into their boat. Billy had a death grip on me when the man suddenly let me go. I fell into the water straight into his arms. I didn't understand what had happened to make the man let me go but we saw the men rowing their boat back to shore. What was going on? Why would they let me go? They knew that they would eventually overpower Billy since there were three of them. They looked past us and we turned to follow their ghostly stares. Ms. Byrtle was standing at the mouth of the cave and she was pointing at them. She looked scarier than I have ever seen, but her looks were not intended for us. We saw Sam crawl to the edge of the cave and motion for us to come to him. We knew that it was the right thing to do because she had led us through our dreams. We swam toward them and he and Ms. Byrtle pulled us up to the safety of the cave. "Witch! You witch! You are supposed to be dead!" We heard the men yell as we followed her through the cave. We went along splashing through puddles until we reached a waterfall that had caves opening up on each side. She led us straight to the falls and behind it into a larger cave. I was so tired and gasping for air. Billy noticed my struggle and secured his arm around my waist. I let out a small yelp of pain but I assured him that I would be fine. We continued trotting behind Ms. Byrtle as the piercing in my side was almost unbearable. "A light. Billy, I see a l…ight." I struggled to say. "Charli, stay with me, please. We are safe now. We only have a short ways to go." I don't know if it was the pain in my side or the thoughts of home that made tears well up in my eyes, but I couldn't stop them anymore. I wouldn't give up now, I had to give it my all and make it to the light. As the light grew brighter, the tunnel grew smaller and dryer. Then the smell, it was the sweet familiar smell that I had always loved. "Charli, your side feels gooey. I am sure that it is bleeding. Can you keep going? I can carry you the rest of the way." Billy told me. "No, I'm fi…" The dim tunnel began spinning as I collapsed in his arms. "Charli, talk to me. Come on, girl. Please." He pleaded, but I couldn't bring myself to respond. "I got you. I will take care of you, I promise." I could hear his trembling voice which made me try harder to stay awake. I didn't speak, I just held him tighter. I relaxed a little and the smell got stronger. It was candles, incense that I smelled. We were getting close to Ms. Byrtle's shop. How could it be possible? Heck, anything was possible in this nightmare. "Put her down on this cot." She told Billy. The cot was about the size of a twin bed and was comfortable enough. "Billy, Where are we?" I mumbled. "I am not really sure, but it's a small room with shelves filled with little bottles. The bottles are filled with different colored liquids." He said close to my ear. "What? I've been here before when I came to get medicine for Sam." I whispered back to him. "Ms. Byrtle needs to check your side." He said as she came back in with a clean cloth that had been wet. She gently lifted my shirt and I heard the boys suck in their breaths. "It is pretty deep, but I think we can get it fixed up. First, we must clean it and make sure nothing is in the wound." She said as the boys sat and listened not sure what to think. Ms. Byrtle had never had much to say to us and we just prayed that one wasn't setting us up for doom. We had to believe that she was really protecting us, but we had no choice at the moment. She worked as gently as she could but the pain was excruciating. She had cleaned the wound but I figured that it needed stitches. "If she needs stitches or anything we will make sure she gets it. We probably should get her over to the doctor's office before infection sets in and she gets a fever." Billy was telling her. "Do you have an antibiotic to give her? I can hold her up if you want to give it to her." He continued as she walked out of the small room. "Charli, I am going to slide my arm under you and lift you slowly. Sam, reach around her on the other side and help me so that I don't hurt her." As Sam reached over and slid his arm under me on the other side, I felt this warm tingling in my side. Both boys froze and stared as Ms. Byrtle entered the room with an odd smile on her face. I completely opened my eyes looked down at my side to see it was miraculously healing. "What is happening?" I asked. "Which one of you has it?" Ms. Byrtle asked and we all looked at her confused. "One of you must have it for that kind of healing to take place." She continued. We stared at her honestly not knowing what she was talking about. "The green stone! Which one of you has it?" We sat there with our mouths gaping open and speechless. "Boys, have a seat, because this is a long story." She pulled up a stool and began, "It all began hundreds of years ago with pirates, yes, real pirates raiding ships and looking for treasures. These oceans have been crossed by queens and kings who have lost millions of dollars worth of jewels. They have been traveled by explorers like Ponce de Leon who spent years looking for the Fountain of Youth, Marco Polo and the Palaces of gold, all the way to Captain Morgan and Silver. All of these men were searching for something and most of it was treasures. I believe some of these treasures were real and are still hidden. Well, today's pirates may not look like the ones we know from history, but they are still raiding ships and hunting treasures. I am sure you witnessed some horrible events on that ship because I know them personally. I have witnessed first hand how dangerous they really are. My ancestors were explorers that came upon this strange land with these strange people, obviously we know now that they were tribal people. My family did not raid their homes, take their lands, or kill them. My family just wanted to share cultures with them. They spent many years and generations with this certain tribe bringing them new items from the civilized world that they knew nothing about. There was a whole different world across that big ocean that they didn't understand, so we brought some of it to them. What my family learned from them was love and appreciation of the land and caring for one another. After a while a young woman from my family had taken ill. She had a high fever and was hallucinating when their shaman placed a green stone in her hand which instantly healed her. No one in my family had ever witnessed any type of magic or whatever you want to call it. Some people call it a miracle." As she paused, everyone looked down at my side. "When my family crossed back over the ocean, they were raided by pirates who found the stone and were completely mesmerized by the sight of it. They took the young girl and the stone and sailed away. Sometime during the night, the tribe members attacked the pirates and rescued the girl as she was returned to our family. We were forever grateful and spent the next years with them. With more and more bad people hearing about the stone, we knew we must leave and never go back because we didn't want to lead anyone to the tribe and hurt them. There are two stones, the one you have, and the one the girl passed down through our family." Sam broke in her story and asked, "How do you know those men who took us?" She answered by finishing her story, "Their captain is a descendant of the bad pirates who captured the young girl with the stone. He knew the story just as I do from our families. We crossed paths forty years ago and the stone had been passed to me when I was twenty. He attacked my family. He killed my brother and tortured me for answers that would lead him to the stone. When I wouldn't tell him where the stone was he left me for dead. He had his men bury me on an island, the same one that he took you to." Billy and I exchanged looks and he said, "We dug up a grave but the box was empty."

"Well, thank goodness for that or I wouldn't be here telling you this story." She said with a light giggle. "Or save our behinds," added Billy. We all enjoyed a quick laugh. "So where is your stone?" Sam inquired. She looked down like she was a little embarrassed then slowly reached her hand to her face. We held our breaths not sure what to expect then with trembling fingers she pulled the patch from here eye. "Oh!" We exclaimed at the same time. An exact replica of our green stone took the place of Ms. Byrtle's eye. "Ms. Byrtle, did those men gouge out your eye during the torture?" I asked as I tried to choke back tears. "Yes, dear they did gouge out my eye among other things. I think the worst part was being buried alive. I was supposed to die, but by some miracle, I didn't." She smiled with the gentlest smile and I knew the boys were feeling the same shame that I was. We had made fun of her by calling her Madame Scary and running from her shop, but now we knew her as who she really was. "The stone works according to who owns it. If that person's heart is good then the stone works good deeds like healing, but if a person is bad then it helps with evil deeds. That is why we have protected it for so many years even given our lives to keep it hidden. We can never let it get into their hands, no matter the consequences." We all looked at the green stone. "Wow! So, can they get to our village?" I asked. "No, not without the stone and they are a little afraid now that they have seen me. They obviously think that I am a witch that has risen from the grave." At the word witch, we turned red. We knew that we were guilty of thinking she was a witch at one time, but she acted like she didn't notice and continued her story, "I do make potions, but I use them for good. I make lotions for skin problems and medicines but I never make anything to hurt anyone. I may use crow's blood every now and then, if I find one already dead but that is all." With that she glanced over and smiled at me. I knew that she didn't throw that bird against my window, but she had taken it to her shop. We sat a little longer before Billy told us that we had better get home to our families. I had been so engrossed in her story that I had almost forgotten about going home. Almost! "What do we tell them?" I asked. "You don't have to tell them too much right now, because I have filled them in on most of the story. The will just be glad that you are home safely. Come back and see me when you have settled in and I will tell you more about the green stone," she explained. Before we could thank her or say a word, Ms. Byrtle disappeared from the room. We slowly walked through the curtain to her little shop and out the front door. Weeks had passed and we suddenly were overwhelmed with emotions. We walked hand and hand through the village knowing our lives would never be the same. I had the two best friends in the world. We had risked our lives for each other and saved each other too.

We slept and slept and slept. We may have taken time to eat a little, but most of all we slept. Then for some reason we awoke on about the fourth day after we returned home, got up and walked to the beach. The sun was warm and the sand felt like silk on our feet. Billy and I sat on the dock with our toes in the water. I felt his large hand reach over and lace his fingers in mine. I lifted my eyes to meet his incredible green eyes. I am not sure how it happened, but he leaned closer, lifted my chin, and gently kissed my lips.